NATSUKO IMAMURA was born in Hiroshima Prefecture. She has won the Osamu Dazai Prize, the Yukio Mishima Prize and the Akutagawa Prize for her fiction, which in addition to *This Is Amiko, Do You Copy?* includes *The Woman in the Purple Skirt.* She lives in Osaka with her husband and daughter.

HITOMI YOSHIO is Associate Professor of Global Japanese Literary and Cultural Studies at Waseda University. She received her PhD from Columbia University, and specializes in modern and contemporary Japanese literature with a focus on women's writing and literary communities. She is the translator of Ichiyō Higuchi, Midori Osaki, Natsuko Imamura, and Mieko Kawakami.

THIS IS AMIKO, DO YOU COPY?

NATSUKO IMAMURA

Translated from the Japanese by

HITOMI YOSHIO

PUSHKIN PRESS

Pushkin Press
Somerset House, Strand
London WC2R 1LA

Original text © Natsuko Imamura 2014

Original paperback edition published in Japan by Chikumashobo
Ltd., 2014. English translation rights arranged with Chikumashobo
Ltd. through The English Agency (Japan) Ltd.

English translation © 2023 Hitomi Yoshio

The lyrics to the song 'Ghosts Aren't Real' (*Obake nante inaisa*) were
translated by Emma Karl-Yoshio, the translator's seven-year-old daughter.

First published by Pushkin Press in 2023

Series Editors: David Karashima and Michael Emmerich
Translation Editor: Elmer Luke

Pushkin Press would like to thank the Yanai Initiative for Globalizing
Japanese Humanities at UCLA and Waseda University for its support.

▇▇ YANAI INITIATIVE

1 3 5 7 9 8 6 4 2

ISBN 13: 978-1-78227-979-2

Designed and typeset by Tetragon, London
Printed and bound in the United Kingdom by Clays Ltd, Elcograf S.p.A.

www.pushkinpress.com

THIS IS AMIKO, DO YOU COPY?

WITH A SMALL HAND SHOVEL AND A CRUMPLED PLASTIC BAG in her hands, Amiko stepped out the back door of the house. For the past couple of nights it had rained, making the path so muddy that her sandals had to be peeled off the ground as she walked, but this morning, thanks to yesterday's sun, they met no such resistance. The mud on the edges of her sandals had hardened gray. She'd run them under the faucet after she's done picking the violets, she decided. Amiko passed the overhanging eaves along the side of the house and walked up the short, gentle slope to the field, where she saw white azaleas blooming by the side of the road. She stopped and wondered if she should pick azaleas instead, but without sturdy shears to cut the branches she decided to settle on the violets after all.

Normally the slope was overgrown with weeds, but last week a kind monk from the temple nearby came over with a mower and made it nice and trim. It didn't feel prickly to walk on anymore, and in appreciation Grandmother gave the monk some sweet green dango dumplings she'd rolled by hand.

Amiko walked up the short slope to the small field where Grandmother tended the cucumbers, eggplants, daikon, and herbs that were planted each year. Snow peas were in season from spring to early summer, and recently they'd been appearing at breakfast, lunch, and dinner, in every dish from stews and soups to stir-fries. Amiko was getting tired of them. She walked past the flat green pods hanging on their vines, averting her eyes, and continued toward the thicket where a persimmon tree bore small fruit every other year.

There, in the reddish-yellow earth, violets bloomed. It was always shaded and damp under the leafy persimmon tree, but perhaps because the soil was rich with nutrients, wild violets thrived, their flowers a vivid dark purple. Amiko wedged her shovel into the earth and dug up the flowers by their roots. When she tried to slip them into the plastic bag, she couldn't find the opening. Her right hand was holding the shovel and her clumsy left hand was of no use, so she used her back teeth and her tongue to open the bag. With shaky hands that made the petals tremble, she slid the shovel into the bag and slowly pulled it out, the handle straight up. She patted the roots and the soil from the outside of the bag so that the stems would be upright. Then, with a "one, two, three", Amiko got back up.

On her way down the hill, Amiko saw little Saki-chan coming toward her on stilts. She was so far away, the size of a pea, but it had to be her. Perfect timing! Amiko waved her hand, which was still holding the shovel, and shouted, "Hey!" There was no response. Perhaps her voice didn't carry, or perhaps she was too far away for Saki-chan to see her. Even if she'd heard her, she couldn't wave back because her hands were clutching the stilts. Saki-chan was making steady progress forward, but moved so slowly that it seemed like she was just stamping her feet in the same spot.

Saki-chan lived nearby and went to the local elementary school. Whenever she came over to Amiko's house, she would appear on stilts. Amiko, who didn't know how to use stilts, was amazed and impressed by her persistence—the house was at least fifteen minutes away walking normally. The little visitor was always delighted when she arrived and was treated to sweets and juice, or was given flowers to take home. A few days ago, on the footpath between the rice paddies, Saki-chan had found some pretty yellow flowers that Amiko knew were toxic. Amiko tried her best to say no, she couldn't have them, but Saki-chan begged. This was unusual, so Amiko gave in and snipped four or five flowers and wrapped them in newspaper for her. The next day, Saki-chan came back—on stilts, as if it were a ritual—with a glum look on her face. "My mom got mad and made me throw the flowers away. She said they were dirty," Saki-chan pouted. "And she blamed you for it, Amiko. I'm so sorry..." She pressed her palms together and bowed sheepishly. Amiko told her not to worry. After all, it was Amiko who had given her those toxic flowers. But the little girl was truly sorry, bowing over and over, her eyebrows arched downward, feeling she'd done Amiko wrong and ready to burst into tears. Amiko decided that the next time she saw Saki-chan, she'd give her flowers that would make her mother happy. That was why she had come outside to pick the violets.

Amiko felt that she should be good to her friends. If Saki-chan came to see her on the days she didn't have school, it probably meant she was fond of Amiko. Amiko was fond of her too. Whenever Saki-chan asked her to do something, like make a big *yeee* grin with her teeth clenched, she would do it. Saki-chan was fascinated by the dark hole that appeared in Amiko's mouth, which was missing three front teeth. To be exact, it was the left middle tooth, the one to the left of that, and the one to the left of that. When Saki-chan first noticed it, she cried out, "What the heck?!" and laughed so hard she could barely cover her mouth with her hands. Then she asked Amiko how it happened. Amiko told her that in junior high school a boy punched her in the mouth and her teeth went flying, which surprised Saki-chan so much she bent over backward. Amiko went on to say that the boy was named Nori and that she'd been in love with him since she was little. Saki-chan, who had a crush on a soccer boy, wanted to know what it was like to be punched in the mouth by a boy you were in love with.

Amiko didn't know how to explain. She wanted to, but it had all happened when she lived in a house far away, before she came to live with Grandmother. She didn't remember much from those days.

"That's boring," Saki-chan complained. But she was captivated by the gaping hole in Amiko's mouth and moved in close for a better look. That was easy enough. Amiko could show her the dark hole as much as she wanted. *Yeeee*. She made a big grin.

ONE

AMIKO GREW UP AS THE SECOND CHILD IN THE TANAKA FAMILY until the day she moved out at the age of fifteen. She had a father, a mother, and an older brother who became a juvenile delinquent.

Back when Amiko was in elementary school, Mother taught a calligraphy class at home. The classroom was small and simple, with three long rectangular tables arranged in an eight-mat tatami room where Mother's mother used to sleep. Now the floor was covered with a red rug from corner to corner. Next to this room was the so-called Buddha room, where the *butsudan* was placed, and across the hall was the kitchen–dining room. The classroom was connected to a veranda, and that's where the calligraphy students entered after removing their shoes. Mother had wanted it this way. Otherwise, if the students entered through the front door, they'd have to walk past the Buddha room and the kitchen–dining room and they'd see into the family's living spaces.

In front of the veranda was a small yard, where Father parked his car. Whenever the car was there, the students had to step sideways in the gap between the car and the concrete wall of the house to get to the veranda, which resulted in Father's navy-blue car getting scratched by the metal snaps on their school backpacks. When that happened, Father never complained but would apply a cream onto a sponge and rub it over the scratches, which made them vanish without a trace. "It's a magic sponge," he would say. Amiko begged Father to let her use the magic sponge, and from then on she would inspect the car daily for scratches before anyone else could discover them and rub them out with great enthusiasm. As a result, Father's car always glistened. But some scratches were deep, and no magic could remove the words AMIKO THE FOOL. Amiko tried valiantly to rub it out—"I almost got it," she said, checking from different angles—but the etched words were never completely gone.

Amiko was in the first grade and could read her own name, but not the kanji for FOOL. When she asked Father what it said, he pushed up his glasses and replied, "Hmmm... I dunno."

The next day, the navy-blue car was covered with a thick rain cover, which remained in place rain or shine.

Amiko missed the thrill of rubbing out scratches, but there were plenty of other fun things to do—like peeking into "the red room" (she called it that because of the red rug) when Mother was teaching a class. Amiko had been strictly forbidden to enter the classroom, so she had to be sneaky. How exciting this was. Yelling "Pee! Pee! Pee!", Amiko would pretend to go to the toilet, tiptoe into the adjacent Buddha room holding her breath, and pry open the sliding doors to create a tiny gap. Sneaking looks into the red room with her left eye, she would see the back of Mother's head, her long black hair pulled tight into a ponytail. Beyond, she would see students facing her way. Around the same age as she was, they were lined up in front of the tables, sitting upright on the floor with their legs tucked under properly. Her brother Kota, who was two years older, was one of the students. He had good posture and was holding a brush. Amiko didn't know any of the other students, but she couldn't resist the temptation of their whisperings and the alluring scent of ink mixed with the smell of newspaper they used for practice. The smell somehow made her want to pee for real, and she would have to go back and forth to the toilet after all.

One summer day, Amiko hid behind the sliding door as usual, occasionally slipping away to go to the toilet.

At one point, Amiko went into the kitchen and returned with a piece of corn cob that Mother had prepared for her. She got into position and began gnawing off one kernel of the sweetcorn at a time, when she noticed that a boy was looking directly at her. He was sitting perfectly still with a brush in his hand, staring at Amiko with big round eyes. The glass door to the veranda was slightly open, creaking gently as the breeze blew in and ruffled the boy's bangs, which glowed in the evening sun. The only other sound to be heard was the crunching of the yellow kernels of corn, which echoed deeply in Amiko's ears.

The boy put down his brush. He picked up the sheet of paper from his desk, turned it around, and raised it up to his face. Written on the white sheet was こめ, the kana for *komé*, meaning rice. The calligraphy was neatly spaced and beautiful, so much more than Amiko's writing. Then, perhaps because the boy had dabbed his brush too deeply in the ink, a drop began to form on the bottom edge of こ. It looked like drool trickling down from a smiling mouth. As Amiko watched, spellbound, the cob of corn in her hand grew hotter and hotter. Her overgrown fingernails dug into the kernels and penetrated the cob. Sweet juice oozed out, mixing with the sweat of her hands and becoming sticky. Her mind became foggy, filled only with the vision of the boy before her.

Then, suddenly, someone shouted, "It's Amiko!"

The students all looked up at once.

"Amiko is watching us!"

One of the boys stood up, full of energy. He straightened his arm and pointed the tip of his brush toward her. "Tanaka-sensei, she's right behind you!"

Mother's head of black hair whipped around, and in the next moment her eyes, narrowed and pointed, landed on Amiko.

As Mother approached, Amiko glanced up at the mole under her chin. "But I didn't go inside," Amiko protested. "I was just looking!"

Mother stepped into the Buddha room, closed the sliding door behind her, and let out a deep sigh. She said to her daughter, "Go to the other room and do your homework."

"Noooo!"

"Don't argue. Hurry up and do as I say."

"But I wanna learn calligraphy too."

"You will not."

"I will too!"

"No one can learn calligraphy until they finish their homework."

"Then I'll just watch."

"You will not. You may learn calligraphy if you can do your homework, go to school every day, listen to your teacher, get along with your friends, and behave yourself. Can you do that, Amiko? Can you promise not to sing in the middle of class or scribble on the desk? Can you promise not to pretend you're a boxer, or walk around barefoot at school, or eat curry rice with your hands? Can you do that? Can you?" After saying all that in one breath, Mother noiselessly opened the sliding door to the red room where her students were sitting, stepped inside, and shut the door in Amiko's face.

It was a while before Amiko realized that the boy she'd seen in the red room that day—the boy who'd written こめ and lifted it up to show her—went to the same elementary school as she did and was in her class. Amiko often skipped school, so she hadn't made the connection. When she recognized him at school one day, she exclaimed, "You're the boy with the drooling kana!" He fixed his round eyes on Amiko for a moment, then turned away.

Later, it occurred to Amiko that maybe, on that day, the boy had been showing his calligraphy to Mother, his teacher, rather than to her. But instead she took it to be a show of affection that was meant for herself alone. During recess, Amiko asked her homeroom teacher how long the boy had been in her class. "Nori?" the teacher replied. "He's been here the whole time. Even before you transferred to this school." That was news to Amiko. "Nori," she said the name aloud.

The first time Amiko said a word to Nori was toward the end of autumn. From the scratchy old loudspeakers at the community center came the familiar tune of

"The Seven Children", which was the sign to everyone playing outside that they should be going home. Kota was walking a few steps ahead of Amiko.

"It's a grave. Amiko, hide your thumbs!" Kota yelled out. He would say this whenever they came by the cemetery, and Amiko would usually get her thumbs out of sight right away, but on this day she was too preoccupied—with Nori—to do so. She'd noticed that Nori had been walking behind her since she left the school gate, keeping a certain distance from her, and so she turned around every two seconds to make sure he was still there. No matter how many times she looked, Nori was there, with the same expression and at the same distance. The same face, the same silky bangs, the same round eyes, the same small mouth as when he showed her his kana for *komé*—all of that was within five or six steps of her.

"It's the stinky church," Kota called out when they approached the small, dilapidated church. "Amiko, hold your nose!" Normally Amiko would respond, "Got it!" and put her hand up to her nose, but today the hand remained by her side. "You listening?!" Kota kicked a pebble and turned around. "Oh, hey, Nori."

Nori smiled at Kota and raised his hand. Amiko

looked at her brother, then at Nori, then at her brother again. "Nori, you're here just in time," Kota said, and ran over to him. They saw each other every week in the red room, of course, as Mother's students. "Do me a favor, will you? Can you walk with my sister for a bit? I gotta go find my friend to give back a manga. I'll be back right away, OK? Catch up with you soon." Kota quickly disappeared into a narrow alleyway.

Amiko and Nori looked at each other for a few seconds, still keeping a distance of five or six steps. Amiko had never been alone with Nori before. Four months had passed since that summer evening in the red room, and the water from the faucet in the schoolyard was cold and tasty now. Winter was approaching.

Amiko turned around to face the road and took a giant step forward. Then she stopped, putting her two feet together. When she looked back, she saw that Nori had also taken a step forward and was about to stop. She took two more steps forward and looked back. When she saw that Nori had also taken two steps forward and stopped, she flashed a big smile and shouted, "I see you, Nori!" Then she turned and started walking. After ten steps, she turned around again and shouted, "I see you, Nori!" with a big smile on her face.

Amiko repeated this again and again. Each time she turned around, she felt happy to see the same face at the same near distance behind her. She was so absorbed in looking backward and forward between Nori and her long shadow that she didn't notice the scenery had changed.

"I see you, Nori!" How many times had she repeated the phrase?

"What?" Nori finally opened his mouth and spoke.

Amiko felt an uncontrollable wave of excitement, as if the insides of her body were bursting at a high pitch. "I see you! I see you! I seeee you!" she shouted, bouncing up and down on one foot. When that foot got tired, she bounced up and down on her other foot. Then she lost her balance, almost falling over, and giggled, "Whoopsies!" When she turned around, she saw no one behind her.

Everything was suddenly still. The melody of "The Seven Children" had stopped. The traffic sounds had stopped. Amiko found herself standing alone on a dimly lit road, about the width of a school hallway. It was a dirt road, but the color looked unfamiliar against her pink sneakers. She was in a strange, new place. The road was lined with white walls on both sides, and in front of them were signs that were stuck into the ground, written in black ink: DON'T PICK FLOWERS, DON'T PICK FLOWERS, DON'T PICK FLOWERS. But no flowers were in sight.

It didn't occur to Amiko that she was lost. She simply thought her body was unable to move. She was stiff from her toes to the top of her head, and her shoes were stuck to the ground. It felt like a long time went by. She clenched her fists and stood still, like a stone, when she began to hear the sound of someone running. The sound was coming toward her, gradually but forcefully. When she cautiously turned her head in the direction of the sound, she was surprised that she could do so with ease. The footsteps were vigorous, and as the ground seemed to vibrate, she clenched her fists more tightly.

"There you are!" It was her brother, Kota. "I've been looking all over for you."

Amiko thought Kota had burst through the white walls that seemed to stretch forever. He was panting heavily, as if he'd been running for his life. He looked around. "Where's Nori? Where'd he go?"

Amiko couldn't answer. When she saw her brother, she felt her stomach heat up, and the warmth surprised her. She started to cry. Kota didn't ask why she was crying, but instead kept looking around for Nori.

"I'm right here."

The voice came from behind them, which caused Amiko and Kota to turn around at the same time. And there was Nori, calmly standing behind them.

"Hey, where were you?" Kota asked.

"I went home to drop off my school bag," Nori answered, empty-handed. "My house is right around here."

"What are you eating?" Kota asked.

"A steamed bun."

Chewing with his mouth half full, Nori wandered off again and quickly reappeared with a steamed bun in each hand. He gave a bun first to Kota, and then to Amiko.

"Why's she crying?" Nori asked, giving her a sideways glance.

"Dunno," Kota replied as he bit into the bun. "Hey, Amiko, stop that crying."

"Not much tears coming out," said Nori.

"That's how she cries," said Kota.

"Oh, weird."

"This tastes great. Did your mom make it?"

"Yup. Hey, why's her voice so low when she cries?"

"You mean Amiko's? Is it low?"

"Yeah, super-low."

"Mmm, this bun is real good. You got any more?"

"What's she sad about?"

"Who knows."

"You don't know?"

"Maybe she tripped and fell."

"Oh yeah?"

"Yeah, probably. Hey, Amiko, you fell earlier, didn't you?"

They took her silence to mean yes.

The steamed bun that Nori gave Amiko had some diced sweet potatoes on top. Amiko tore them off and gave the rest to Kota.

The tasty sweet potatoes and the fact that Nori had spoken to her, even if it was only a word, made Amiko feel closer to him than ever. She would walk home with him every day if she could. But that was Kota's responsibility, and almost never did anyone join them.

It was also Kota's duty to make sure Amiko didn't

misbehave. Amiko enjoyed walking to and from school with her brother, but maybe he didn't feel the same way. He wouldn't let her hold his hand, and he often told her "shut up" or "quit it". Sometimes she'd be going on about something and he'd suddenly grab her arm, pull her around a corner, and tell her sternly to "stay still". That happened mostly when Kota's friends were coming toward them.

In those situations, Amiko had to hide with Kota until his friends had passed. "They're gone!" she would whisper, and Kota would take a peek, look around, and continue walking with more swagger than before. Once, he emerged too quickly after Amiko's all-clear and was spotted by his friends, who came up to them and circled around Amiko.

"Whoa, it's the sister. Kota's little sister."

"You're Amiko, aren't you?"

"You're the one who eats lunch with your hands!"

So word had gotten out about Amiko and her habit of eating curry rice with her hands. Whenever she did that at home, saying, "Look, I'm in India!", Mother would have a fit.

Kota didn't say a word while his friends clustered around Amiko, or after they left. When they passed the cemetery and the church, Amiko waited for his usual orders to hide her thumbs or hold her nose, but on that day he was silent. It was the same when an ambulance drove past them. He didn't remind her, even though ambulances were bad luck, so Amiko forgot to hide her thumbs. She worried that something terrible would happen and told herself to be a little more careful when telling her brother the coast was clear.

One evening, as Amiko was lying on the floor watching cartoons on TV, Father asked if she thought she'd be able to walk home from school by herself from now on. "Uh huh," she mumbled, still engrossed in the cartoon. Then, shortly after, Kota came in holding a cup of jello and a spoon. "Here you go," he said, offering it to her, and Amiko reached up to take it just as the program switched to a commercial. The jello was filled with fruit that looked like red jewels—they were cherries, Kota's favorite. Amiko scooped up the cherries and put them in her mouth, and handed the cup back to Kota. Turning her attention back to the TV screen, she slowly chewed on the soft cherries and decided that, starting the next day, she would walk home with Nori.

Still, Amiko could count with her fingers the number of times she got to walk home with Nori. Whenever she shouted his name at the end of the school day, he would run out of her sight. Or sometimes she was so preoccupied with the cartoons and snacks that were waiting for her at home that she forgot all about Nori and would hurry home alone. But when she had something important to tell him, she would look for him until she caught him, and they would walk home together surrounded by noisy classmates. On these occasions, Nori would pull down the brim of his school cap until it covered his eyes and bite down on his lip.

And so it was, the day after Amiko's tenth birthday. Walking next to Nori with his cap pulled down over his eyes, Amiko told him excitedly all about the previous night, from the presents she received to how delicious the dinner was.

On the evening of her birthday, Father gave Amiko a set of toy walkie-talkies at the dinner table. They were the same kind that her favorite cartoon characters had, and she'd been begging for them for a long time.

"I can play spy with the baby!" She jumped up and down in excitement. The baby was Amiko's soon-to-be-born brother or sister.

Father also gave her a box of heart-shaped chocolate cookies, a pot of yellow flowers, and a twenty-four-exposure disposable camera. "You can take pictures of the baby with this," he told her.

Amiko was thrilled to get the camera with the shiny green packaging and kept turning it over to look at it from different angles. "Can I practice?" she asked.

"Sure," Father replied. She broke the seal, and with Kota's help turned on the flash. She held up the camera to take a photo of the family.

"Wait a minute," Mother interrupted. She got up from her seat, her arms around her large belly, and brought a hand mirror from another room. As she began arranging her bangs, the dinner table grew quiet. Father reached for some pickled cucumbers with his chopsticks and crunched down on them. Kota, on the other hand, was frozen in place, his fingers made into peace signs, waiting with a silly look on his face.

Amiko stared through the lens at Mother, who kept fiddling with her bangs. The middle part of her face was hidden by the hand mirror, but Amiko could see, from under the mirror, a mole the size of a soybean clinging to the left side of her chin. Mother's fingers kept arranging and rearranging her bangs. Unable to wait any longer, Amiko pressed the shutter button. When the flash went off, Mother looked up from the mirror and turned toward Father. "I can't believe it," she said. "Didn't I just tell her to wait?"

"Hmmm," Father mumbled.

Amiko raised the camera again and called out, "That was practice. The next one's the real thing. Are you ready?"

"That's enough," Mother said sharply and turned her back to the camera. "No more pictures. Amiko, please stop."

Father, refocusing on the meal, picked up a wooden spoon and prepared to dig into the egg custard in front of him. The silly look on Kota's face faded, and the peace signs he was making with his fingers curled inward.

"I'm gonna take another one. Everybody, look at me!" Amiko called out to the family. No one turned to look at her.

"Thank you, Amiko. That will be enough," Mother said, taking the camera out of her hands and placing it on top of the refrigerator. She then opened the lid of the rice cooker and served Amiko first in her flower-patterned bowl. It was rice pilaf with vegetables and meat—Amiko's favorite dish. Mother was such a good cook, she knew exactly what everyone liked. When Amiko took a bite, the savory flavoring was so delicious that she declared, "I know I'm gonna have seconds!"

But Amiko, who ate like a bird, couldn't even finish the small bowl before her. With two or three bites left, she threw her pink chopsticks onto the table. Mother tried to offer her some karaage fried chicken, another favorite of hers, but Amiko shooed away the plate, saying, "No more." She then grabbed the box of chocolate cookies that Father had given her and placed it on her lap. "This is what I'm having!" she announced excitedly as she opened the lid with a big heart on it. After licking the chocolate coating off the surface of every cookie, she felt so full she could barely breathe.

Amiko had thoroughly enjoyed the evening. She wanted to tell Nori everything.

"Guess what? It was a gray one!"

"Wanna see it?"

"It stretches at the top."

"Oh, and a camera too."

"I took a picture of Mom."

"The flash and everything."

"Let's play with the walkie-talkies, okay?"

"Worms."

The conversation was all Amiko talking. Nori didn't say a word, but that was as usual. He could be chatty and boisterous with his classmates, but alone with Amiko he was always silent.

"Chocolates. Oh, and flowers, too."

"Are you jealous?"

"I'm gonna take pictures of the baby."

"Walkieee-talkieee."

There was the ring of a bicycle bell, and a woman she'd never seen before rode by with a smile on her face. "Hi there, Amiko," she called out to her.

"Good afternoon, ma'am."

It was Nori who greeted the woman as she rode away. He was silent with Amiko, but when an adult happened to pass by he would have something to say.

Hearing Nori's voice pleased Amiko, and, clearing her throat, she took out a box from her bag.

"Here you go, eat this," she said, handing him the box.

"What is it?"

"Wow, he talked!"

"What is it, I said."

"Chocolates. The ones I got yesterday."

"The ones from your birthday?"

So he'd been listening, even though he hadn't uttered a word.

"Yup. You can have 'em. Eat up."

"I don't want 'em. My mom would be furious if I took them home."

"Then eat 'em now."

"Now?" Nori opened the box. "Hey, these aren't chocolates," he frowned, then reached for a wheat-colored biscuit and began to bite into it. "What's chocolate about this? These are cookies."

"Yummy, right?"

"They're stale."

"But yummy, right?"

"They're okay. They're stale."

Nori ate every single cookie in the box. When he was done, he threw the empty box toward Amiko, which landed by her feet. She picked it up, satisfied.

After waving goodbye, she tucked the box under her arm and skipped all the way home. "That's not skipping," Kota might have said if he'd been with her.

"Amiko, that's not skipping, that's stamping!" Kota had once told her. It had been one of those evenings when all the sounds that filled the small town seemed to come from far away, like they were an illusion. Amiko had looked up and seen a cloud descending from high above the roof. What was left of the midday sun came through the flat cloud, making everything appear golden. Amiko, who was wearing a white sleeveless dress, had jumped up to pick a red fruit hanging from a tree.

Amiko didn't know what "stamping" meant, but Kota was laughing so happily that she skipped all the way home. It was funny to her too, because she could barely move forward. Kota had been always two or three steps ahead of her. But on this one evening, he walked slowly and leisurely behind his sister as she skipped.

Back then, Kota still smiled. But it was so long ago it seemed a miracle that he ever did. Since he became a juvenile delinquent, Amiko never saw him smile and couldn't even remember what that looked like.

It all happened suddenly. There was only a before and an after, and Amiko couldn't recall anything in between. It wasn't just Kota. Mother changed around the same time too. Just as Kota transformed from a normal boy into a delinquent, from one day to the next Mother lost all motivation in her life.

TWO

IT WAS DECEMBER, ABOUT THREE MONTHS SINCE AMIKO HAD received the set of walkie-talkies for her birthday. By then, Mother was teaching calligraphy with a very large belly. Students would ask to touch her belly, and she would smile and let them do so every time. From behind the sliding door, Amiko once watched as Nori placed his hand on the belly and shouted, "It moved!" Mother would sometimes let Amiko touch her belly in the kitchen, but she would quickly move away, saying, "That's enough." It was never long enough to feel the baby moving. The belly simply felt hard, warm, and round. When Amiko tickled the belly and asked, "Does the baby feel me tickling?", Mother only replied, "Hmmm,

I wonder..." She couldn't tell if Mother was happy or sad.

Amiko was ecstatic the day Mother told her she was going to be a big sister. She couldn't help thinking about it from morning till night. *I'm gonna be a big sister. A big sister! What'll we do together? What toys will the baby like?*

Kota was excited too. "I hope it's a boy. When the baby boy comes out, we're gonna play ball together," he told Amiko many times. Amiko didn't like to play with anything resembling a ball, so she wouldn't be able to do that, but she had the best toy—the walkie-talkies. She and the baby brother would play spy with her shiny silver walkie-talkies. Her heart raced with excitement.

On the baby's due date, Amiko decided it'd be good to try out her walkie-talkies so she'd be prepared when the baby came home. Outside would be best, but it'd been raining since morning and was freezing cold, so the practice run had to take place indoors. She handed a walkie-talkie to her brother, who was upstairs in his room, and asked him to go downstairs to test things out. He didn't tell her that it was only the baby's due date, not the day the baby would come home—or that even if the baby did come home that day, it would be a long time before the baby could use a walkie-talkie. But Kota was game. "All right, let's try it!" he exclaimed as he took the walkie-talkie and ran down the stairs. That was before he became a juvenile delinquent.

Once Amiko was sure Kota was downstairs, she pressed the talk button. Her whole body seemed to brighten up with the touch of her index finger. She took a deep breath and sent the first message.

"Do you copy? Do you copy?" She called out to her brother, who stood by on the lower floor.

There was no answer.

"Awaiting reply. This is Amiko. This is Amiko. Do you copy?" There was a crackling noise, but still no reply. "Hello. Hellooooo? Do you copy?"

As Amiko patiently waited, she started to hear what sounded like a faint voice amid all the grating noise. She wasn't sure whether the voice was coming through the walkie-talkie or directly into her ears. But it didn't matter. What Amiko heard was her brother's voice, and then suddenly Father's. Father was supposed to be at the hospital with Mother, but he had come home. The baby was born! Amiko instantly popped up, opened the door of her room, and shouted: "Dad, you're home! Is the baby here?"

Breathing heavily, full of excitement, Amiko was running down the stairs when she heard the front door slam. Kota was standing alone in the hallway.

"Where's Dad?" she asked her brother breathlessly.

"He went back to the hospital."

"Oh. Where's the baby?" she asked, looking around.

"...The baby's not here."

"Where is it then?"

"Nowhere."

Kota walked past Amiko with his head down, went quietly up the stairs, and closed the door to his room. In his right hand he still held the walkie-talkie.

As Amiko stood alone, the hallway felt hard and cold. Her breath was white even inside the house. The only sound that could be heard was the crackling noise from the walkie-talkie in her hand.

Large flakes of snow were falling on the day Mother came home from the hospital. Amiko was waiting outside, melting icicles on her tongue and catching snowflakes in her hands. She had waited outside for so long that when Mother finally arrived in Father's car, her "welcome home" greeting sounded like a clattering of her teeth. Still, Mother understood. "I'm back," she said, and took Amiko's hand. This startled Amiko and she tried to pull away, but Mother wouldn't let go. She wrapped her hands around Amiko's, pressing them tightly together, and whispered, "Your hands feel like ice."

It felt strange to be touched by Mother. Amiko had never been hugged or caressed by her before, not even hit or dragged around. She didn't dislike the feeling, but she kept looking back at Mother's hands on hers and then at her pale face, wondering why the sudden touching. Then she noticed that Mother seemed to have become smaller. Not only the belly, which had flattened out, but the whole Mother, even the mole under her chin. "Let's go in quickly—we'll all catch a cold," Father said, and so the three of them hurried toward the house. Mother kept holding Amiko's hand until they walked through the front door. When Amiko looked up at Mother's face again, she felt a large snowflake fall onto her eyelid. She shook her head and batted her eye, wet and cold from the snowflake. Amiko heard a tender voice above her say, "Oh my, oh my."

Everyone said the whole business with the baby was very sad. People stopped Kota and Amiko on the street, telling them again and again how sorry they were. Keep your spirits up, they said. Each time Amiko would reply, "I know, it's such a bummer," while Kota would mutter in a low voice, "Um, yeah... sure."

At home, Amiko was busy caring for Mother, who couldn't move around much after returning from the hospital. She put on a *kamishibai* storytelling picture show that she scripted and drew herself, and brought juice and snacks to Mother in bed. When Amiko performed a magic trick where a rubber band jumps back and forth between her fingers, Mother was so impressed that she wanted to learn how to do it herself. So she decided to teach her the trick every day. It was the first time she had taught Mother anything. When Mother finally mastered the trick, they called Father to show him. "Wow, that's amazing! You two can be a magic mother–daughter team," he laughed, and applauded. Then Mother raised her hand with the palm facing Amiko. Amiko didn't understand what this meant, but she raised her hand in the same way. The two palms met—the mother's and the daughter's—making a nice clapping sound. It was Amiko's first high-five.

When the snow that remained on the roads finally melted away, Mother suggested to Amiko that they go for a long walk. The wind was still cold but the sun felt warm, as if spring had arrived. They walked leisurely toward a place where there was already the smell of grass. When they arrived at the riverbank, Mother laid out a picnic sheet and sat on it, as Amiko busily picked a bunch of wild plants—*yomogi* mugwort and *tsukushi* horsetail. Then, after a while, Mother exclaimed, "My goodness, it's already three o'clock," and unwrapped the bento they had prepared. The rice balls, wrapped in seaweed, were oval-shaped, which was how Amiko liked them. And then there were little sausages, braised burdock, macaroni salad, and rolled omelet. The carrot slices were cut out like flowers, which Amiko had helped make.

"Thank you, Amiko, dear," Mother said rather suddenly, as they were eating strawberries for dessert.

"For what?"

"For being so kind. Kota is kind, too. And so is Dad."

"Oh yeah?" Amiko said, picking off a strawberry leaf stuck to her tongue. "Kind?"

"Everyone is kind to me. I'm so grateful."

"Kind, huh?" Amiko mumbled, as Mother looked at her with smiling eyes. She reached for her third strawberry.

Mother held up a pair of orange plastic chopsticks that she'd been using.

"Kota gave me these. He told me I should use these to eat lots of good food and get better. Mom is so happy to use these chopsticks from Kota and to eat the bento you helped Mom make."

These days, Mother referred to herself as "Mom". It had always been "I" since the day they first met.

"Amiko, dear, when we get back home, why don't we make tempura with the *yomogi* you picked? Dad will love it."

"Okay!"

"You'll help me?"

"Yeah."

Mother smiled.

It soon grew cold. Mother took out a wool sweater from her bag and put it around Amiko's shoulders. Amiko didn't want to go home yet, so they agreed to stay until they found a four-leaf clover. They continued sitting on the picnic sheet, picking at the grasses around them and chatting about whatever came to mind.

"Maybe it's time to start the calligraphy class again," Mother said.

"Let's do it!" Amiko responded, pumping her fist high in the air.

For the last three months, the Tanaka Calligraphy Class had been closed. If the class reopened, Amiko thought, Nori would come to the house every week. Of course, she could see him at school, but the teachers were always scolding her so she spent most of her time napping in the infirmary or reading manga in the library. Plus, if Nori was at her house doing calligraphy, she could see him in action, when he was most attractive. "Is it okay if I watch?" she asked Mother.

Amiko remembered Mother's face and voice from before as she told her: "You will not." But this time, Mother said with a smile, "Oh, Amiko, you're going to learn calligraphy too. Even though I'm your mom, I won't go easy on you. I hope you're ready for it."

Amiko was surprised. She was going to be Mother's student! When she looked up at Mother, who had been smiling all day, she saw that her mole, which had looked so small on that cold winter day, was now back to its original size. It shook under her chin whenever she laughed.

And so it was decided that the calligraphy class would resume in April when the new school year started.

—

Amiko was now in the fifth grade, and no longer in the same homeroom as Nori. So at the end of the first day of school, Amiko ran to Nori's class and shouted from the hallway.

"Hey, yoo-hoo, Nori! Calligraphy class is starting today! Did you know? Yoo-hoo!"

Nori only looked down.

"Miss Tanaka, is it you again? Be quiet, please, we are still in class," Nori's homeroom teacher said sternly and glared at her. At that moment, some kid in the class piped up in a loud voice, "It's Amiko!"

"Gross, did you see that? She threw him a kiss."

"Eeew, a kiss! Whoa, she did it again. To Nori!"

"Hey, Nori, what's this about? Is Amiko your girl-friend?"

Nori shook his head vigorously and shouted something back.

"Amiko's in love with Nori. Amiko wants to marry Nori!"

"Everyone, stop it. Be quiet."

"Barf! That's... so... gross...!"

Whaack! The class fell silent. Nori looked down, biting his lip so hard it seemed like blood would burst out at any second.

Amiko decided to wait quietly in the hallway. As soon as the afternoon assembly was over, she ran up to Nori, who came out of the classroom with his cap over his face. She could hear the teasing and whistling coming from all around as she walked next to him, but the further they got from the school gate the less the noise could be heard. That was when Nori said, "Today's not my calligraphy day."

"Wow, he talked!" Amiko shouted.

"Hey, you hear what I said?" Nori turned his head to look at her, only the tip of his nose and mouth visible.

"Yeah. I just wanted to tell you that it was starting today. That's all."

"You didn't have to wait for me."

"Oh, I did. Today you're gonna write something for me."

There was a reason why she'd been waiting.

"Huh? Write for you? Write what for you? You're making no sense."

"Want me to tell you?"

"No."

"I'll tell you."

"No thanks." Right after he said that Nori, who was wearing his cap too far over his eyes, walked into a telephone pole. Amiko laughed. He turned around, holding his forehead with one hand.

"Hey, just so you know, I'm only doing this because my mom tells me to," he said. "*Kota's sister is a little weird, but don't bully her. Watch out for her if she does anything strange.* That's what my mom tells me, and that's why I walk home with you. To tell you the truth, I hate it. Hey, what's so funny? What? Tanaka-sensei's baby didn't make it, right? You shouldn't even be laughing."

"But that was too funny! And the baby did make it. The baby was born."

"That's not true."

"The baby was born, but he was dead."

"That's not called being born."

Amiko had never heard Nori talk so much. He was talking to her, and to her only. She was so happy that she couldn't stop laughing and skipping around. "Hey, write me something," she said, tugging at Nori's sleeve.

He shook her off. "I told you today's not my calligraphy day."

"No, not calligraphy. I brought you something to write on. Here."

Amiko pulled out a wooden sign from her bag. It was attached to a stick that was covered with dirt like a fresh vegetable. When Nori turned it over, he saw the words, DON'T PICK FLOWERS. He lifted the brim of his cap. His round eyes finally emerged.

"This came from the Yokotas' place," he said. "What... what do you think you're doing? They're going to get mad when they find out."

"Here, write on this: BABY BROTHER'S GRAVE."

"You got to be kidding."

"My baby brother's dead. I wanna make a grave for him."

"You're such an idiot. Go away."

The sign was going to be a gift for Mother, who finally decided to reopen her calligraphy class. The night before last, as Amiko was watching TV, Kota showed her a weird-looking carved wooden doll he had made. "I'm gonna give this to Mom. You should give her something too."

Amiko asked him what she could give her. "Anything," Kota replied. "Mom's been depressed ever since the baby died. Now that she's finally going to start teaching again, we should do something nice to celebrate."

When he mentioned the baby, Amiko got an idea. Mother had once told her that the graves she had made for her pets—GOLDFISH GRAVE and TOM'S GRAVE—were dirty, so this time she was going to make a beautiful one that wasn't dirty at all.

She remembered the wooden sign from that day she got lost on the unfamiliar road, right by Nori's house.

"Please, Nori, you gotta help me," Amiko begged. She *needed* Nori to write the letters. She couldn't think of anyone else who could write as beautifully as he could. She begged him again and again, but he wouldn't give in.

"No way."

"Please, please, please. I'm begging you with my life."

"Would you stop it?" He began to walk ahead of her.

"It's for Mom. It's for her celebration."

Nori stopped in his tracks. "What, a celebration? For Tanaka-sensei?"

"That's right. Two nights ago, he told me to give Mom something special as a celebration."

"Who told you that?"

"Told me what?"

"To make a grave for her. Who told you? Your dad?"

"No."

"Kota?"

"Yup."

Nori silently took the sign and the magic marker in his hand.

The words that he wrote, BABY BROTHER'S GRAVE, were so beautiful that Amiko could not stop staring at them. They looked even better after she took the sign home and put animal stickers all over it. Then, after admiring the sign for a long time, Amiko went to the corner of the yard where there were several planters. Next to the one with scallions growing was a bare planter where her goldfish and Tom—the *kabutomushi* horned beetle—had been laid to rest. The planter was a bit crowded, but it would have to do.

Mother was preparing dinner when Amiko went up to her and said, "Hey, Mom, I wanna show you something."

"What are you up to, dear?" Mother said, smiling. Mother used to speak only in standard Japanese, but recently she'd begun to mix in some Hiroshima dialect when she talked. Amiko thought it was funny because this was new and different.

"Come outside for a minute," Amiko said, tugging at the sleeve of Mother's blouse.

"Outside? OK, but I'll need to turn off the stove." Mother let Amiko pull her sleeve and hurried into the hallway, her slippers flapping. "Oh, Amiko, you didn't come to the red room today. Where were you?"

"Out."

"I was worried you didn't like calligraphy anymore."

"No, that's not it. I'll come tomorrow."

Amiko had had her first calligraphy lesson in the red room a few days before the class reopened. Mother, standing behind her, placed her veiny hand over her daughter's holding the brush. Lifting the small hand within hers, she soaked the brush in ink and wrote slowly, stroke by stroke, on a white sheet of calligraphy paper. Downstroke, up-flick, full stop, now relax your arm... Amiko didn't know what she was writing. Her invisible right hand, fully controlled by Mother, drew lines, dots, bars, and curves in black ink, as if all on its own. Rather than being parts of a character, the shapes emerged like puzzle pieces that fitted automatically together before her eyes. Only Mother knew what the finished picture looked like. On the top half of the sheet of paper, the kanji for *ki*—希—was completed. Now put down the brush and take a deep breath... Then they took up the brush again and repeated the dicing motion of the strokes on the bottom half of the page. It was the kanji for *bou*—望.

"Together the two characters—希望—read as *kibou*," Mother said. "It means hope."

When Amiko looked back at Mother, she was surprised at how close her face was. It was so close the mole under her chin almost touched her.

"Hope is Mom's favorite word," Mother said, but Amiko's mind was too preoccupied by the mole to hear.

"Where are we going?" Mother asked as she followed Amiko out the door.

"This way! This way!"

The sun was setting. From the kitchen next door came a vigorous sound of something frying in a pan.

Amiko stopped and pointed. "Here it is."

"What is it?" Mother bent down to see.

It was getting dark, but not so dark that the words were illegible. Mother brought her face closer to the

sign wedged in the planter alongside GOLDFISH and
TOM. Amiko waited for her response, practicing her
whistling while Mother was stooped down. But there
was nothing. Mother seemed to have become frozen
in place.

"Isn't it nice?" Amiko called out to her. "Hey, isn't it
real nice?" She was sure Mother would be impressed
at how nice the whole thing was.

"I made it myself. There's no dead body inside
though."

Mother crouched down with her back to Amiko and
began to cry. At first, Amiko thought she was cough-
ing. She was making a high-pitched, croaky sound.
Then it turned into what sounded like a moan, then
eventually something much louder. Mother's crying
echoed piercingly, and Kota came running out the
front door. "What happened? Amiko, what happened
to Mom?"

"Dunno. She just started crying."

"Why would she... Wait, what's this?"

"What?"

"...What is this?"

"This? It's a grave."

"It's Nori's handwriting."

"Yup."

Father was back from work. "I'm home," he called out.

Kota ran over to Father with the sign he had pulled out of the planter. "Look at this... this... prank..." Words stumbled out of his mouth. Father glanced at the sign and walked toward Mother, who was bent over and still whimpering. He tried to help her up but she wouldn't move, so he put his hands under her arms and had to almost drag her inside the house. The woman next door opened her small kitchen window to watch what was going on. Kota turned and glared at her, and she shut the window quickly. Kota kept glaring at the window, motionless, then slowly turned toward Amiko and asked in a low voice, "Amiko, did you ask Nori to write that?"

"Yup."

"You asked Nori to do it?"

"Uh huh."

"Why?"

"Nori has great handwriting."

"No, I mean, why'd you make the grave?"

"The baby came out dead. He needs a grave. Plus, it's for Mom's celebration."

"Did you think Mom would be happy about it?"

"Why wouldn't she be?"

"She was crying, didn't you see?"

"Yeah, but that came out of nowhere. I didn't do anything, I swear."

"Amiko."

"What?"

"Amiko."

"What?"

The sun had now set. Kota looked in pain. He opened his mouth and closed it, opened his mouth again and closed it, and finally turned away without saying anything.

A few hours later, Nori was brought to the Tanaka home by his parents. Amiko turned off the TV so she could listen to their conversation, which took place by the front door. She could hear Father's high-pitched voice saying, "It's not all his fault" and "It was just a childish prank." She also heard Nori sobbing, which continued from the moment his family rang the door-bell until the moment they left.

The next day, Nori came to school with red eyes. When Amiko went up to him, he kicked her in the stomach. "It's your fault I got in trouble," he spat.

But Amiko didn't get in trouble. No one scolded her anymore.

From that day on, Mother lost all her motivation.

It was around the same time that Kota suddenly became a juvenile delinquent.

One day, when Amiko came home from school, the house reeked of something awful. It wasn't ink or newspaper or food she didn't like—it was something new. That something made the house feel strange, like it wasn't her own. Amiko went to Mother to find out the cause. "Mom, what's that awful smell?" she asked.

Mother was focused on stirring the pot of miso soup on the stove and didn't answer. That evening, Amiko asked Father the same question.

"Looks like Kota took up smoking," he answered matter-of-factly.

"Whaaaaat?" Amiko ran up the stairs and burst into Kota's room.

Kota was sitting cross-legged on the floor, flipping through a magazine. The room was a mess. Amiko dove at him: "You started smoking? You a smoker now?"

"Shut up," Kota said, and pushed her away.

"You smoke. That's what Dad said. You smoke. That smell..." Amiko lunged at him again. This time, Kota pushed her so hard she flew out of the room and banged her head on the wall. She screamed in pain.

"Leave me alone, you pain in the ass!" Kota yelled, slamming the door as she cowered in the hallway.

"You're crazy. I can't believe it. You... you..." Holding her head in her hands, Amiko called out to Father downstairs. "Dad! Dad!"

There was no response. Amiko wanted Father to knock some sense into Kota, but that didn't happen. When Father did speak to Kota, who was starting to smoke at the age of twelve, he simply told him to be very careful about putting out the cigarettes.

Kota joined the local motorcycle gang. He hung out with the gang all day and stopped talking to Amiko altogether. He rarely came home, and when he did he demanded money from Mother. He would barge into the red room in the middle of calligraphy class and yell, "I need money!" When Mother shook her head, he would grab the tuition envelopes that had just been collected and storm off.

One day, Amiko was watching this happen from behind the sliding door. The envelope that Kota grabbed had just been handed to Mother by Nori, who was one of the few students who still attended the class. The enrollment had declined dramatically due to Mother's loss of motivation. Amiko was supposed to be a student now, sitting in the red room with the others, but she still preferred peeking, as she would often do on the days when Nori attended the class. In fact, Amiko had not picked up the calligraphy brush since the day Mother took Amiko's hand in hers and wrote the kanji for "hope".

"Not that one... No, no!" Amiko shouted, jumping out from behind the sliding door and clinging to Kota. Nori, sitting upright with his legs tucked under him, watched Amiko with his mouth wide open. But Kota didn't seem to realize it was his sister. In fact, Amiko wasn't focused on her brother either. She was throwing punches at Kota's stomach, but her eyes were fixed on Nori, who was holding a brush. On the desk before him was the sheet of paper on which he had been writing his beautiful characters. What were the kanji he'd written? In her distraction, Amiko could do little to stop Kota, who stormed off undamaged.

Amiko, feeling defeated, sighed and looked over at Nori, who was hurrying to leave.

No one came to the house for calligraphy lessons after that. But even before the incident, Amiko had heard students whispering and saying things like, "Look, Tanaka-sensei's sleeping standing up!" or "She doesn't care anymore."

With calligraphy class ended, Amiko hardly had a chance to see Nori. The school year drew to a close, and most of the students in Amiko's school went on to the junior high school in the district. Amiko did too, and she was surprised to learn, two months into the new school year, that Nori was in the same class as she was.

THREE

WHETHER AMIKO WENT TO SCHOOL OR NOT DEPENDED ON HER mood that day. Mother had stopped speaking almost completely by then, so there was no one to tell her to go to school or to do her homework. Father left for work before Amiko woke up and came home late at night. On rare occasions, she would see him at the dining table reading a newspaper and would ask him to play cards or the Othello board game with her. He never did.

"Go play with Kota," he would say without looking up. But Amiko had no idea where her brother was or what he was doing.

Kota was going to the same junior high school as she was. Amiko was in the first year, and Kota, who was two years older, in the third year. It wouldn't have been surprising if they passed each other in school, but she never saw him around. Still, everyone knew who he was.

Not long after the entrance ceremony, a group of girls Amiko didn't know took her into the school bathroom and took turns kicking her in the shin. "What a nice sound she makes," they said.

As the girls took turns kicking her, another girl burst through the bathroom door. "Stop! That's Tanaka-senpai's little sister. You know, that guy in the third-year class."

The girls froze. They stopped the kicking and changed their tune, suddenly making nice. "We're sorry. We made a mistake." "We didn't know." "You don't look like him at all." "Did it hurt? It didn't, right? Not that much?"

Amiko nodded.

"Don't tell Tanaka-senpai, OK?" the girls said, each flashing a smile, and ran off.

After that incident, Amiko often heard Kota referred to as Tanaka-senpai with respect or maybe fear. One day, a classmate was making fun of the *shitajiki* writing pad that Amiko had been using since elementary school. It was illustrated with the anime Zen monk character Ikkyu-san. When she mentioned that her brother had given it to her and that he had drawn Ikkyu-san's nose hairs himself, the classmate grew quiet, and then a moment later said, "Wow, Tanaka-senpai... he's so good at drawing." The classmate didn't tease her anymore.

— "*Shhh*, it's Tanaka-senpai's..."

— "You better be careful around her."

— "When Tanaka-senpai loses his temper..."

— "That's Amiko, right?"

— "Mess with her, he'll beat you up."

If this mysterious Tanaka-senpai was in fact Kota, Amiko thought, they knew more about him than she did. Even Nori was referring to him in the same way. Once, when she was walking down the hall, she heard him telling some friends, "You know, Tanaka-senpai and I go way back. We used to take calligra—" Then he stopped. One of the boys had whispered, "It's Amiko... over there! She's looking at us!"

Nori was always surrounded by his friends, so Amiko never had a chance to talk to him even though they were classmates. What was he starting to say about calligraphy? Was he going to tell his friends about the red room? If so, she wanted to hear all about it too.

Thanks to Mother's weekly teaching all through elementary school, Nori's calligraphy now stood out from everyone else's. One day, the teacher posted the students' calligraphy sheets on the back wall. "Which one is yours, Nori?" Amiko asked, but he ignored her. So she asked another boy who was passing by. The boy took a quick look at the wall, then flicked a certain sheet with his finger, which made a clucking sound. The kanji *geshi*—夏至—were written on it.

"Wow," Amiko sighed.

"What? What is it?" the boy asked.

"It's amazing."

"What's so amazing about the kanji for summer solstice?"

"Nori's handwriting. It's so beautiful."

"Uh... yeah, compared to yours."

Amiko's sheet was not on the wall. She might have skipped class that day, which would not be unusual. The boy pointed to another sheet and said, "Look, this one's mine."

His calligraphy was no good. She quickly turned her attention back to Nori's.

*   *   *

One morning, Amiko was asleep in her room upstairs when she was awakened by the wind shaking her window, making a steady, rustling *cluck, cluck, cluck, ssh ssh ssh*. The curtains had a vertical stripe pattern of pale blue and white, which did little to block out the strong summer sun. Squinting, Amiko picked up her broken alarm clock and found that it was almost ten o'clock. She stretched in her futon, brushed away the hairs stuck to her face, got dressed, and left for school.

The next morning, Amiko woke to the same sound. It was long past time for school, but she put on her wrinkled uniform and left the house without washing her face, as she had done the day before. The sound of the wind woke her up again the next day. And the next. She heard the same sound every day. Not only in the morning, but also in the afternoon and in the evening, even when the wind wasn't blowing. Amiko opened the thin curtains and peered out at the small balcony. There was nothing except for a few empty flowerpots pushed into the corner. She ran down the stairs and stepped into the kitchen, where Mother was at the dining table, face down, asleep. Her long hair was no longer pulled into a ponytail but sprawled out in all directions, as if gushing from the top of her head. "I'm hearing something weird up there," Amiko reported to the hair.

Mother didn't lift her head. She seemed to be fully concentrated on sleeping, and may not have heard Amiko's voice. She tried again. "I'm hearing weird noises up there and no one's around."

No response. She gave up asking.

A few days later, Amiko got a hold of Father and told him, "There's all these weird noises coming from the balcony outside my room."

"Oh yeah?"

"It could be a spirit. I saw something on TV about that the other day."

"Oh, yeah? That sounds scary."

"Yeah, they showed a guy who was possessed."

"Scary. Very scary."

Cluck, cluck, grrr, ssh ssh ssh ssh ssh, brrr brrr. Amiko soon noticed that the strange sounds were not just coming from the balcony, but that they could be heard anywhere if she listened carefully enough. She heard them even when she pressed her fingers against her ears. Soon, she heard them on her way to school and in the classroom. "You hear them too, don't you?" she said to a girl in her class. "Shhhh, listen! There it is."

The girl frowned and said, "Creep." No one wanted to listen to the sounds Amiko was hearing. No one could hear them but her. It was just like the psychic special on TV. Only those who could see could see, only those who could hear could hear. Most people didn't feel the presence of the spirit. Amiko wished the sounds would go away, but the more she wished, the louder they got.

The sounds continued. One day, either in the first or second year of junior high school, Amiko was staggering down the hallway when she saw Nori coming toward her. It was probably in the second year because she felt she hadn't seen him in a long time. Nori had grown taller and his hair was longer, which made him look all the more handsome. "Nori!" she exclaimed as she approached him.

Nori stepped to the side to avoid her, but Amiko grabbed his sleeve. "Listen, on my balcony, there's..." Nori shook her off. A girl who had seen this exchange yelled out, "Eew, gross!" and another boy shouted, "Run, Nori! Run, run!", clapping his hands. Nori ran. "Run away! Amiko is coming after you!"

Amiko didn't run after Nori. She watched as he ran away, away from the whirlpool of laughter.

One autumn night, Amiko walked downstairs with a blanket over her head. It had been too noisy to sleep. The strange sounds, which were muffled at school, were the loudest from the balcony of her room. She had tried closing her eyes tight, but that only made her head hurt.

Normally, on the days she skipped school, Amiko had a regular routine of eating snacks, reading manga, watching TV, and taking naps, while doing some made-up exercises in between. But her energy was so depleted by the lack of sleep day after day that even those activities felt like a burden. At school, the boy sitting next to her asked if she was taking baths. She thought about it but couldn't remember the last time she'd taken one. "I'm gonna be real. You stink," the boy told her.

It all started with the sounds. Amiko felt so weak that she lost all energy to eat and bathe. It was difficult for her to keep track of time, and she was regularly tardy or absent from school. On several occasions, she would arrive at school with her hair all over the place and find out it was already time to go home. But, for some reason, no one scolded her like they used to when she was little.

When Amiko opened the door to her parents' bedroom, it was dark and quiet. She lay down quietly in the corner near the door.

When she woke up, she was back upstairs in her own room.

She could still feel the ache in her left shoulder where her father had shaken her awake a few hours earlier. Wrapped in a blanket, in a daze, she was forced to stand and go up the stairs one by one. *Right foot, left foot, right foot, left foot, right foot.* Father's voice echoed in her ears as he steadied her to be sure she wouldn't fall backward. Then he pushed her into her room and closed the door.

The next time Amiko stepped into her parents' bedroom, she announced, "I'm gonna sleep here from now on, okay?"

The bedroom was crammed with two futon mattresses, which covered almost the entire floor space. Mother seemed to be asleep with a quilt over her head, and Father, having just gotten out of the bath, was sitting on his futon, drying his hair with a towel.

"Why?" he asked.

"I've been telling you," Amiko replied. "There's a spirit up there."

"Go to Kota's room then. There's plenty of space there."

"His room stinks. I don't wanna go in there."

It was only when she wanted to borrow manga that Amiko entered her brother's room. She would hold her breath and run out as soon as she got what she was looking for. He was never in the room, but there was always the bitter, syrupy stench that came from the old pineapple tin can he used for an ashtray.

"You watch too much TV, Amiko," Father said. "You're just imagining things."

"No, I'm not," Amiko replied quickly. And then she told Father what she'd been thinking for some time. "I think it's the spirit of the baby."

Father stopped drying his hair.

Amiko continued, "You know, the baby that died." Father stood up. "It's been a long time, but I bet he's still in this world, looking for a place to rest." Father glanced over at Mother, who was sleeping under the covers. "Dad?" Amiko said, looking up at him.

Father approached. With his right arm outstretched, he gave her a firm push on her left collarbone. She stumbled back, and he pushed her once again on the same spot. And before she knew it, Amiko found herself standing outside her parents' bedroom.

"That's it. I can't take it anymore," said the boy sitting next to Amiko. It was independent study period, and the classroom was noisy. Amiko couldn't quite make out what he said, but he seemed to be talking to her. "Take a bath. Seriously, please."

"Mmm..." she mumbled.

Then the boy kicked the leg of her chair hard, and the chair tilted sideways with Amiko sitting on it.

"Whoa!" He cried out in surprise. "You weigh nothing. Do you ever eat?"

Amiko shook her head.

"Then eat something. You're all skin and bones. It's gross."

Gross was a word she heard a lot in junior high school. She heard it more often than good morning.

"Look. Your brother graduated. Do you understand what that means?"

Her brother graduated. That was news to Amiko, but why was he suddenly bringing up her brother?

"Wake up. Everyone left you alone last year because they were scared of him. Without your brother, you would've been dead meat. Now you never come to school, and when you do show up, you stink. Seriously, someday, they're gonna come after you. You don't want that, do you?"

"Uh huh."

"Not *uh huh*. They're gonna stomp all over you. Is that what you want?"

"No."

"Well, then, at least take a bath. And eat something."

"Okay."

"And what's up with the bare feet? What happened to your school shoes? I mean, you're not even wearing socks."

His eyes were on Amiko's feet. When she arrived at school this morning, she found that her indoor school shoes were missing from her cubby. She wasn't wearing any socks, so she'd been barefoot since morning.

"I couldn't find them. My socks are at home."

"What if you get your feet stepped on? That's gonna hurt like crazy. You'll cry. Want me to try? Here we go... Just kidding. Or what if you stepped on a thumbtack? OK, let's do an experiment. We'll try it right here, right now... Just kidding. Ha ha ha, you idiot. But you know... Actually, it's kind of nice, when you think about it. It's like you're free. Well, it's also why you get bullied..."

The boy went on and on while looking now at Amiko's legs—they were as thin as burdock. He was very talkative. Amiko felt like talking too, about something she hadn't told anyone in a while.

"Hey, guess what," she said. "There's a ghost on my balcony."

"Huh?" The boy raised his head to look at her.

"It's been there for a while now. I hear all these weird noises even though there's no one around."

"What kind of noises?"

"It's really getting on my nerves. It's so loud."

"Well, what kind of noises?"

"Um, it's like this. *Cluck cluck, psss, grrrrr, kurr kurr, psssss, pur pur, brrr brrr brrr brrr.*"

"OK, shut up already. It's annoying. Hey, let me see your worksheet." The boy grabbed the sheet of paper on Amiko's desk. "Whoa, what's up with the kanji?" He started flicking his fingers at all the mistakes. "You don't need any kana after *watashi*—私. If you write *shi*—し—after it, then it's gonna be *watashi-shi,* like 'me me'. And look here, the left side is all wrong in *asa*—朝. For 'morning', you have to write 卓, not 車. That would be *kuruma*—'car'. Your handwriting's pathetic, too." Then he turned to her and sighed, "You really need to smarten up."

"Uh huh," Amiko replied.

"You didn't study much in elementary school either, did you? If you keep skipping school, you'll never get into high school."

"Uh huh."

"And why is your handwriting so bad when your mom's a calligraphy teacher? Well, you were never in the room, I guess. She used to scold you every time you tried to come in. She'd give you the mean eye just for peeking from behind the door."

The boy knew a lot.

"It's partly my fault, I guess. I can tell you now— my friend and I used to have a competition going. Who can spot Amiko first? The first one to shout, 'It's Amiko!' got 100 yen. Not just in the calligraphy class. At school too."

"Oh."

"Maybe we overdid it."

"You were in the calligraphy class?"

"What? Of course I was. Take a look at my handwriting. Isn't it good?" The boy held out his own worksheet to show her. It wasn't good at all. "Hey, so, this balcony. Do you mean the one where you guys used to hang the laundry and dry persimmons and stuff, or the narrow one on the other side of the house?"

"What?" At the mention of the balcony Amiko looked up from the worksheet.

"The ghost. You said there's a ghost."

"What ghost?"

"You gotta be kidding me. You just said there's a ghost on your balcony."

"Oh, yeah. I hear weird noises when nobody's there. *Psss psss psss psss, cluck.*"

"Yeah, you said that already. Well, it could be a spirit."

"That's what I think too. So... what do I do?"

"How should I know?"

The bell rang to signal recess. Amiko left the classroom carrying her empty school bag. The hallway felt nice and cool against the soles of her bare feet, making a pitter-patter sound every time she took a step. Then, to the rhythm of the steps, out of nowhere, some melody and lyrics she'd heard before began to play in her head. There were still classes left after the ten-minute break, but Amiko suddenly felt hungry and decided to go home. It had been a long time since she felt hungry.

That night, Amiko sang. It was the song that came flooding into her head that afternoon in school. When she sang at the top of her lungs, she realized she could no longer hear the spirit. Father came into the room and said to her, "Sing more quietly, will you? Mom is sleeping." She lowered her voice. Singing in a near-whisper, she began to hear the engines in the distance, the motorcycle gang running wildly through the city at night. She lowered her voice even more and listened carefully while humming through her nose. *Yup, that's him.* There was one that was especially loud. That one was leading the pack, roaring powerfully and pulling along the other motorcycles that followed. All the others struggled desperately to keep up, determined not to be left behind. Amiko followed along. Her voice grew louder and louder with each pull, as the growl of the engine came nearer. Her singing turned into shouting, she ranted and raved, and when she felt like the top of her head would burst open, she heard Father yell, "Amiko!" She pulled the covers over her head.

From that day on, Amiko was no longer bothered by the strange sounds. It didn't mean the sounds disappeared. When she approached the balcony she could clearly hear them, but at a distance she didn't hear them anymore. Before, she could hear them wherever she went. The sounds of *grrr grrr, psssss* used to accompany the rhythm of her walking. But no more. She was amazed. She realized that, by singing, she could close up the spaces where the sounds used to enter. So she decided to sing whenever she could, when she was walking outside, sitting in class, at home, or anywhere else. She sang even when she had a cold and her voice was hoarse. On festival days she sang to the sound of the *taiko* drums, and on Saturday nights she sang to the deafening roar of the motorcycles. Singing made her hungry, so she ate snacks, then some milk bread, then a banana. Singing in the bathroom sounded so nice and pleasant that she bathed several times a day.

By the time another school year came around, Amiko was clean and no longer skin and bones.

FOUR

ONE SUNDAY AFTERNOON, AMIKO'S HOMEROOM TEACHER CAME
to visit the Tanaka home. The parent–teacher–student
meeting was usually held at the school, but because Father
couldn't take time off from work on weekdays the teacher
came to their house. None of the usual topics—entrance
exams, career counseling, mock examination results—
were mentioned. At the kitchen table, the teacher didn't
touch the tea or the steamed buns that were offered, but
instead showed concern about Mother's health. "How
is Mrs Tanaka doing?" the teacher asked.

"Well, there are good days and bad days," Father
responded.

"She sleeps all day long," Amiko added, chewing on a
steamed bun. "She doesn't have any motivation at all."

"When she stays at the hospital, she does come back a little better. But it's a mental condition, as you know, so she can take a turn for the worse at any time..."

"What do you mean stays at the hospital? You're talking about Mom?"

"I understand. That's certainly..."

Neither Father nor the teacher looked at Amiko. The whole exchange was taking place over her head. "That's certainly a difficult situation," the teacher said gravely in a low voice, and that was where the conversation ended. After seeing the teacher off at the door, Amiko repeated her question.

"So what's this about the hospital? Who stays there?"

"Mom does," Father answered with his back to her.

It was the first time Amiko learned that Mother had been staying in the hospital. "She does? Even now?"

"She's home now," Father answered, lowering his voice.

Amiko looked in the direction where Mother was sleeping, toward the red room. At some point her parents started sleeping in different rooms, and the red room became Mother's room. Not wanting to disturb Mother when she was asleep, Father forbade Amiko from entering the red room or even the Buddha room next to it. This was why the three-way meeting was held in the kitchen. "Oh okay. I had no idea," Amiko said.

Father had told her that the reason why Mother slept all the time was because she had an illness of the mind. When Amiko heard this, she was surprised that such a disease existed. A full-grown adult, her own mother for that matter, sleeps in her room all day long without cooking or cleaning. No broken bones, no surgery—just ill in the mind. Amiko wondered how Mother could occupy a whole room and even stay in a hospital with a reason like that. Shouldn't Father be scolding her a little? If he pushed her and pushed her until she was back in the kitchen, just like he had pushed Amiko out of their bedroom that night, maybe Mother's motivation would come back.

It'd been years since Amiko tasted Mother's cooking.

"Can you tell me what you like to eat?"

The first time they met, Mother asked this question of Kota and Amiko, who were still young. "Meat," Kota answered. "Me too," Amiko said. Notepad in hand,

Mother wrote down their favorite foods, saying, "Kota likes meat, and Amiko also likes meat..." The light breeze from the fan on the ceiling caused the pages of Mother's notepad to rustle.

Kota and Amiko sat side by side on one side of the table, and Father and Mother sat on the other. Amiko, wearing a white sleeveless dress, had a plate of pancakes with whipped cream in front of her, while Kota, wearing a short-sleeved shirt buttoned up tight, had a bowl of beef stew in front of him. The café had a wide selection of foods, ranging from *takoyaki* dumplings to steak to *anmitsu* dessert. Mother had ordered a sandwich but had barely touched it. "Sayuri's cooking is out of this world," Father said proudly, while mixing his *hayashi* rice.

"I like pancakes too," Amiko added. Mother smiled and nodded. Amiko said again, "I like pancakes too!"

Mother's eyes widened. She picked up the notepad she had placed on the table, and jotted down while saying, "Amiko likes pancakes, too."

"Dad, can I have some ice cream?" Kota asked after finishing his beef stew. Father nodded, and Mother, who was sitting on the aisle side, turned her head to call the waitress walking by.

That was the first time Amiko looked at Mother's face from the side. On the lower left side of her chin there was a mole—a large mole that looked like a black fruit. Amiko couldn't take her eyes off it.

Suddenly she felt a sharp pain on her calf. "Ouch!" Amiko shouted and looked up at Kota, who was sitting next to her. "You kicked me!" He didn't look back at her but kept spooning the ice cream into his mouth.

After leaving the café, Kota and Amiko walked home together. Father and Mother had somewhere else to go.

"She's a mole monster," Amiko said.

Kota gave her a horrified look. "Don't ever say that in front of that person. Not even in front of Dad."

"She's not *that person*. She's Mom."

"Don't ever say that, OK? And don't stare at that person's mole."

"She's not *that person*. She's Mom."

"I know, I know... you understand what I'm saying?"

"That mole looks like it'll fall right off."

"It's not gonna fall off."

"Yes, it will."

"No, it won't. Moles don't fall off."

"They do. I saw 'em the other day."

"What?"

"I saw a bunch on the road on the way to the park."

"Those aren't moles. Those are just beans... or trash."

"No, they were moles."

"That's impossible. Now stop it. If you don't, you're gonna get it."

Kota yelled and pretended to hit her, but Amiko didn't stop. She wasn't lying and she was going to find some moles on the ground to prove it. When Amiko turned around to go her way, Kota grabbed her shoulders and held them firmly.

Looking her squarely in the face, Kota said, "Amiko, that person we just met, she's going to become... our new mother."

"I know. She's gonna be our new mom."

"OK, so... when a kid looks at his parents... or, hmmm, let's say... when a tadpole sees a frog, does the tadpole wonder why the frog is green and croaks?"

"When what?"

Amiko didn't understand what Kota was trying to say, so he changed his tactic. He bowed down toward her, so she could see the top of his head. He ran his fingers through his short hair and revealed a pale area where he was losing his hair. "You see the bald spot?"

Amiko nodded.

"So, Amiko, what am I to you? Am I your brother or am I a bald spot?"

"My brother," Amiko answered.

"That's right. And what's Dad to you? Is he your dad or is he a pair of glasses?"

"My dad," Amiko answered.

"That's right," Kota nodded. "OK, so what about the person you just met? Is she your mother or is she a mole?"

"My mom!"

"That's right. You got it."

Kota nodded his head, his chest heaving with pride. But immediately afterward Amiko exclaimed, "Oh, look! That one's the same size as the mole!", pointing somewhere high up in a tree. Kota sighed.

"You don't get it, do you?"

Amiko was pointing to some red berries on a tree. It was a goumi berry tree planted inside someone's yard, whose branches reached over the fence and hung down heavy with fruit.

Umph! Amiko jumped with her right hand outstretched. Not even close. She showed her palm to her brother. Nothing.

Umph! Even higher... *Umph! Umph!* Come on, try again... *Ooorah! Umph!*

Ooorah! Before long, Kota had joined in the jumping to try and pluck the berries.

Umph!

"No, no, Amiko. It's too late if you try to grab the berries *after* you jump. You have to jump *and* grab them at the same time." Kota jumped high. "Like this!" He landed on the ground and slowly opened his right hand before Amiko's eyes, showing her the contents of his palm. "See?"

In his hand was a fruit that was much larger than it looked from down below.

"I wanna get one too." *Umph!*

"Amiko, you gotta grab *when* you jump. Watch!" She heard a snapping sound as Kota's outstretched hand tore off a thin branch. He planted his feet on the ground. "See?"

Amiko tried again and again to imitate her brother. *Umph! Umph!* She kept trying until the sun began to set, but she just couldn't reach the fruit. As the color of the sky changed from orange to dark blue, the color of the berries changed from red to black. Kota dropped a handful of berries he had picked into Amiko's hands. "For you. They're sweet."

When Amiko plopped them in her mouth, they didn't taste sweet at all. She jumped up and down shouting, "Aaaah, they're sour, they're sour!", until the jumping turned into skipping. "Amiko, that's stamping," Kota laughed as he walked behind her.

True to Father's words in the café, Mother was an excellent cook. Amiko preferred snacks to meals in general, but now that Mother stopped cooking, what she missed was the taste of home-made rice pilaf and braised burdock. She guessed that Father must miss her cooking too. Kota was never home, so who knew how he felt.

"Hey, Dad, let's ask Mom to make us something yummy," Amiko said to Father the night of the parent–teacher–student meeting.

Father was eating a bowl of udon, and Amiko was eating her udon plus a piece of milk bread. They were sitting at the dimly lit dining table where the teacher had joined them earlier in the day. Father didn't say yes or no to Amiko's suggestion but, with his chopsticks still in his hand, brought up a completely different topic.

"Hey, Amiko, what do you think about moving?"

"Huh? What?"

Mother's cooking went out the window. Amiko was confused by the word "moving". Father had never mentioned such a thing before. It didn't make sense to her, and above all she didn't understand why they needed to move. Father continued to slurp his udon and said no more. Amiko tore off a large piece of bread and stuffed it into her mouth. She looked at Father while she chewed, and kept on looking at him until the bread had turned to mush. As she swallowed, the realization finally hit her.

"I get it! You're getting a divorce."

"Hmmm," was all Father would say.

Divorce. That must be it.

A few days later, Father handed two boxes to Amiko. One was for things she needed and the other was for things she didn't need. Things she needed would go inside the pink storage box for the move, and the rest would go into the regular cardboard box and be tossed out. It was a simple task, but the room only got more and more cluttered as Amiko tried to decide what she wanted to keep. Seeing no progress, Father finally came into her room on his day off to help separate her things.

"We're gonna get this done in two hours," he announced, and started throwing whatever he laid his hands on into the cardboard box. Amiko would yell every time he did this and dig her hands inside the box to rescue the junk that had been tossed in it. The task was going nowhere.

"This one's still usable," said Father, tossing something into the pink box for once. Amiko looked to see what it was. It was the green disposable camera.

"I don't want this one," she said.

"There's still film inside. You can use it."

"Don't want it," Amiko insisted, and tossed the camera into the cardboard box. Father reached inside, took the camera out, and threw it back into the pink box.

"Don't be wasteful. You only took one picture, so you have twenty-three pictures left."

"I said I don't want it...!"

Amiko grabbed the camera and threw it as hard as she could against the cardboard box. It made a loud, dull thud on the side of the box and rolled onto the tatami floor.

Father stopped and looked at his daughter for a moment, then turned his back without saying another word. He began tossing the clutter into the cardboard box at a steady pace. He didn't touch the camera again.

Amiko sat and watched what he was doing. But when she saw the next item about to be disposed of, she lunged forward and snatched it from him.

"I need this," she declared. It was the walkie-talkie, now a dull gray. She held it to her chest with one hand and looked around. "Where's the other one? Help me find the other one!"

She shoved Father out of the way and sat where he'd been sitting. Sticking her head into the cardboard box, she rummaged through the contents, pulling out whatever her hands could grab—a bag of old sparklers, elementary school textbooks. Things flew through the air and scattered on the tatami floor.

"It's gone. The other one's gone. There should be two of them. I was gonna play spy with my baby brother. There were two, I swear. It's gone. Dad... did you take it? Dad, you hid it, didn't you?"

Suddenly there was a loud thump. Amiko felt the vibration through her knees. Father had slammed his fist on the tatami, which silenced her. He exhaled deeply, stood up, then said clearly, "There was no baby brother."

The moment Amiko looked up into Father's face, she knew she'd made some kind of a mistake. How many times had she seen that look directed at her—at home, at school, and on the streets? Father was angry. Amiko tried to understand what he said. But why was he angry? He said there was no baby brother. She had to think fast. Father had already gotten up and was about to leave the room.

"But there was," Amiko managed to say. "There was, remember? The baby died and he's stuck in this world. He's still here, even now, Dad. Listen, Dad, you can hear his spirit right in this room."

Amiko reached for the hem of Father's brown sweater and yanked as hard as she could. She tried to pull him to the balcony, but no matter how hard she pulled he wouldn't budge. "Please, Dad. Come. I'm telling the truth, you gotta believe me. *Sssh*. Be quiet, really quiet. I'm not lying, I swear. You can hear it if you listen." The sound, which wouldn't go away no matter how hard she tried, was nowhere to be heard. Had she sung too many songs? Why couldn't she hear it now? Father's sweater stretched and stretched.

"Please, Dad... just listen!" Amiko shouted as if in prayer. Father finally turned his head.

The look of horror on his face was gone. Amiko felt relieved and loosened her grip. The sweater, released from her grasp, snapped back onto his thin body. She felt so relieved that she no longer cared about the spirit. Now they could sit down together and clean everything up.

Father remained standing. His anger was gone, but his voice sounded slightly higher than usual as he said, "It was a girl. A sister."

"Huh?" Amiko was confused. "A girl? The spirit is a girl?"

"No, not the spirit, Amiko. I'm not talking about any spirit." Father's voice rose even higher. "I'm talking about the baby. The baby girl."

"The baby girl?"

"You don't understand, do you?"

"What do you mean...?"

"You wouldn't understand, Amiko."

It took a while for Amiko to process what Father had said. At first, she thought he was talking about the spirit, but that wasn't the case. Then it occurred to her—he was talking about the baby that came out of Mother's belly. The baby that died without ever seeing the light. It wasn't a brother.

Father turned his back again and started walking away.

Why had she thought it was a baby brother? It was a baby sister. No one had told her that. Or had they told her and she had forgotten?

Amiko remembered that she had made a grave. She made the grave and showed it to Mother, who cried when she saw it.

Amiko heard Father's footsteps going down the stairs, and soon she heard nothing at all. Her six-mat tatami room had returned to the state it was in before the clean-up began, with everything strewn across the floor—her clothes, manga, empty snack boxes, textbooks and workbooks that had barely been opened. In the corner of the room lay a walkie-talkie. The one whose pair was missing. She was going to play spy with the baby. How many years had it been since that plan fell through?

One, two, three... Amiko counted with her fingers. The baby girl would be five years old now. The girl she never got to meet and would never ever meet. The girl seemed to stand before her, but had no face. Amiko tried to remember her face. Then she became confused, because she was trying to recall the face of a girl she had never met.

FIVE

WHEN AMIKO OPENED THE DOOR TO THE SCHOOL INFIRMARY one day in February, she was greeted by the heat from the stove and the school nurse.

"Hey there, Amiko. It's you again." The nurse was a middle-aged woman, but she talked like a man. "I'm sure tired of listening to your out-of-tune songs."

"Can I borrow the microphone?" Amiko held out her hand.

"You think this is your private karaoke room, huh?" said the nurse, handing over the toy microphone. Amiko grabbed it, took a deep breath, and started to sing.

GHOSTS AREN'T REAL. GHOSTS ARE JUST A JOKE. This was the song that Amiko sang.

PEOPLE WHO ARE HALF ASLEEP, THEY JUST MADE A BIG MISTAKE.

It was always this one, and this one only.

BUT I AM STILL, BUT I AM STILL, A LITTLE BIT...

Here she lowers her voice.

GHOSTS AREN'T REAL. GHOSTS ARE JUST... A... JOKE!

The last line ends in an explosion.

"I'm gonna go deaf," said the nurse, wrinkling her nose and covering her ears.

School was in session, and Amiko had been taking a math test until a few minutes ago. She had finished and put down her pencil with a lot of time still left, so to pass the time she had propped her chin in her hands and started humming.

Father had already decided when the move would take place. He didn't want to disrupt her education, so the move would happen as soon as she graduated from junior high school. Moving meant that her "future path" was already decided. No teacher, no guidance counselor needed to tell her to study now. Actually, it had been a long time since anyone had told her to study. In the silent classroom Amiko's humming echoed surprisingly well, and someone whispered, "Will you shut up?"

The teacher called out from the podium, "Miss

Tanaka, if you have to sing, go outside and do it." Amiko got up from her seat and left the room.

In the infirmary Amiko could sing as loud as she wanted, and no one got angry as long as other students weren't there too. She knew there'd be snacks and juice, lots of manga, and even an Othello board game if she asked. She felt much more comfortable there than in the classroom.

Amiko finished singing the song and felt she could keep on going. She lifted the microphone to her mouth and was about to sing the song again when the nurse put her palm in front of Amiko's face and told her to stop. There was someone at the door.

"Come right on in," the nurse called out.

When the student opened the door, a familiar face peeked through the gap.

"Oh hey, Nori...!"

Nori didn't look at Amiko. He didn't move an inch from the door, even though the nurse beckoned him to come in. When she asked him what was wrong, he answered properly though in a muffled voice.

"I've been feeling sick all morning, so I was going to ask if I could rest here a bit. But actually, I'm okay. I'll go back to the classroom now."

The nurse stopped him from leaving. "You look pale. Take a rest, even just a short rest. Amiko, you can be quiet, right?"

Amiko nodded energetically. "I'll be quiet. Come in, Nori. Want some juice?"

Nori came in silently, a little wobbly. He sat down slowly on the sofa, placed his arms on his knees, and sunk his head into them.

"You're in bad shape. Studying too hard for the entrance exams?" the nurse asked.

He nodded faintly. Amiko took out a carton of apple juice from the small fridge and poured it into a mug that was drying by the sink. She tried to give the mug to Nori, but he didn't move. Thinking he might want something sweet, Amiko asked the nurse if she had any snacks.

The nurse opened a drawer in her desk and pulled out a box. "I know you don't have much appetite, Nori, but if you get hungry, have some of these. Amiko, don't eat them all by yourself."

The box had a large gold heart at the center, which made Amiko light up. "Oh! I know these. I've had them before." When was that? It seemed like ages ago. "You like these too?" she asked the nurse.

"Sure do. The chocolate coating is pretty good, but the cookies underneath have a nice crunch to them."

"A nice crunch, huh?" Amiko thought for a moment, but couldn't remember how the cookies tasted.

The bell rang. It was time for a ten-minute recess, and the hallway began to buzz with students going to their next class.

The nurse asked Nori if he wanted to rest in the infirmary or leave school early, and he said he would go home. When she stepped out to call Nori's parents, Amiko and Nori were left in the room alone. Amiko stood with her hands clasped behind her back and looked down at Nori. His light-brown hair hadn't changed since the first day she saw him. Because his face was buried in his lap, she could gaze at him to her heart's content. It had been a long time since she had observed him so closely. They'd been in different classes the year before, and though this year they were classmates again, their seats were far apart and they never talked. Minutes before, they'd been taking the same test in the same room. Soon they would both graduate and be worlds apart.

Amiko waited. Nori's head was still in his lap. When he looked up, she was going to tell him that she was moving away. Listening to the rumbling of the heater, Amiko silently called out to Nori to look up at her. She sent him meaningful gazes; but nothing. She noticed a piece of lint on the shoulder of his black uniform and, holding her breath, she gently picked up the lint and dropped it on the floor. He didn't notice.

"Hey, you had some lint on your shoulder," Amiko said softly; again, nothing. "Yoo-hoo, Nori. Good morning." Silence.

With nothing to do, Amiko sat down on the sofa facing Nori and reached for the box on the table. She picked out an individually wrapped cookie, ripped it open, and took a bite of the chocolate heart. Just as the school nurse said, the cookie underneath the chocolate coating was nice and crunchy. Crunch, crunch. "Mmm, these are yummy," Amiko said aloud so Nori could hear.

Amiko reached for a second one. This time, she licked the chocolate off with her tongue and savored the taste. After licking the chocolate clean from its base, a round, wheat-colored cookie emerged. She placed it on the table and reached for a third. She did the same with the third one, licking off the chocolate coating. Then, as if a fog had lifted, Amiko remembered. She knew this taste. She had eaten them before. Father had given them to her for her tenth birthday.

Amiko got up and shook Nori's shoulder.

"Nori, wake up. These are your favorite. Look, Nori, I know you like them!" She spoke loudly, shaking him hard. Nori refused to raise his head, but she wanted him to remember. "We were in fourth grade. I gave you these on the way home from school. The chocolates from my birthday, remember? The ones you really liked. You ate 'em all up."

Nori sat still like a rock. Amiko gave up and sat down again. The bell rang, and the hallway was once again busy with the sound of footsteps clattering down the hall. Then it was quiet. Amiko picked up a fourth chocolate cookie. The sound of her tearing the wrapping echoed through the infirmary. Just as she was about to put the cookie in her mouth, Nori's head shot up, and he let out a gasp that was like someone coming up for air from underwater. He glared at Amiko with bloodshot eyes. She stared back at him in surprise.

"Tell me those were just plain cookies," Nori said.

His voice sounded raspy and faint. Nori looked at the heart-shaped chocolate cookie in Amiko's hand, then at the two round wheat-colored cookies on the table. The two plain cookies were moist, having just been licked clean by Amiko. A shaky voice emerged out of Nori's mouth. "The ones I ate..." he seemed to say, but Amiko couldn't make it out. There was a short pause, and just as Nori opened his mouth to speak again, Amiko shouted, "I love you!"

"I'll kill you," said Nori at exactly the same time.

"I love you!"

"I'll kill you," said Nori again.

"I love you!"

"I'll kill you."

"Nori, I love you!"

Nori's threats had no effect on Amiko. They didn't leave so much as a scratch. Only Amiko's words held the power of destruction. Amiko's words struck Nori, and they also struck Amiko herself. Every time she cried, "I love you!", the words shattered her heart without mercy. I LOVE YOU! I LOVE YOU! I LOVE YOU! I LOVE YO... The moment Nori punched her in the face, his eyes red and boiling, Amiko felt relieved that she could finally take a breath.

* * *

When Father came home and saw his daughter sitting in the entryway with a reddish-black clump of tissues in her mouth, his face turned white. He immediately pulled her into the car and started the engine without a word. On the way, Amiko tried to protest—*Where are you taking me? I wanna go home*—but he silenced her with a voice so angry and terrible that she could hardly believe who it was. "Don't talk," Father ordered, and she did as she was told. The car sped like a runaway roller coaster. It ignored the traffic lights, nearly ran over a girl on a bicycle, and arrived at the hospital before Amiko could even put on her seat belt.

Amiko received three stitches in the upper-left corner of her mouth, where her snaggletooth met the back of her lip. From that day on, she could no longer trace her upper lip with her fingers to feel the tooth beneath it. She lost one snaggletooth on the left, one tooth next to it, and her left front tooth. They had flown out of her mouth in the infirmary, along with blood.

Amiko didn't count how many times she was punched in the face. It couldn't have been that many. Strangely, she felt no pain while it was happening. It was Nori who left the room first. He muttered something under his breath, then ran off. The nurse hadn't yet returned. Amiko left the infirmary soon after.

She had no intention of returning to the classroom. The infirmary was located on the first floor of the school building on the south side, only ten steps to the front entrance. From there, it was another thirty steps to the main school gate. She didn't see anyone as she left the school. On the way home, an old man turned his head slowly as Amiko staggered by. He stood still, supporting his bent back with his cane, and stared at her without saying a word. Then a young woman with a small dog stopped and called out to her, "What happened? Are you all right?" Amiko ran past her as fast as she could. "What happened? Wait!" She heard the woman behind her call out, but Amiko didn't look back. The dog was barking wildly and trying to bite her. When Amiko reached home out of breath, she opened the front door to find a place to sit down. She stuffed her mouth with rolled-up tissues and waited a long time for Father to come home.

Amiko cried after the procedure. She was still crying in the car on the way back home.

It hurts. I wanna stay in the hospital, she tried to say to Father, but all she could manage was a low moan.

Dad, why can't I stay in the hospital?

"Try not to talk," Father replied in his usual voice.

Mom got to stay there, didn't she? I wanna stay there too.

"Try not to talk, I said."

It's not fair. Why does Mom get to have her way and I don't?

It was late and the road was empty. Father and Amiko both wore seat belts this time, and they cruised at the same speed as the cars around them. They stopped at red lights and started again once they were green. At the hospital, he had answered questions on behalf of Amiko, who was unable to speak. "She must have fallen and landed hard on a corner. I'll be sure to ask her what happened later." But he never did.

Because of the gentle, pleasant vibration of the car, in addition to the painkillers beginning to take effect, Amiko soon felt like her head was weighed down by cushions, a weight she wanted to shake off but was too sluggish to do so. Father was taking her home. She didn't care about the hospital anymore. She just wanted to crawl into her futon and go to sleep. She was envious of the person who could be enveloped in a soft, fluffy futon from morning to night. Amiko was sure that even now, in the room that was covered by the red rug, that person was sleeping quietly and peacefully, unaware that her daughter had lost her teeth and so much blood.

Mother lived her life hiding from Amiko. For many years, ever since the day she lost her motivation, her only goal in life seemed to be to avoid being seen by Amiko. Eventually, Amiko could no longer picture what Mother looked like. The only thing she could remember was the mole. Mother's mole was like a black soybean that was always on the verge of falling off, whether she was laughing or crying or angry, whether she was eating or writing. When Amiko first saw the mole it looked huge, like the size of a goumi berry fruit, but that was because she was little. Amiko learned over time that moles don't fall off. Still, for some reason, she continued to be obsessed with Mother's mole.

Kota had told her she shouldn't be so critical, especially with family members.

*　　*　　*

It took four days until the stitches were removed, and by the time three more days had passed Amiko had recovered to the point where she could talk as before. The skin around her lip where she'd gotten the stitches was scarred and stiff, and it sometimes made her drool, but she didn't find it particularly inconvenient. The doctor told her that because parts of her teeth remained, he could put in some crowns using the roots that were still there. But Amiko rather liked feeling the uneven holes in her gums when she traced them with the tip of her tongue. That became a new habit after a while, and she told the doctor she had no use for any new teeth.

SIX

ONE SUNNY MORNING, AMIKO PUT A LID OVER THE PINK BOX.
The box containing all her belongings was light
enough to lift with one hand. When she shook it, it
made a clattering sound. Amiko was ready, with plenty
of days left before the move, which was to take place
the following month.

Shuffling across the tatami on her knees, Amiko
plopped down on the white space softly illuminated
by the winter sun. The junk that had filled the room
was emptied out with the help of Father each time
the garbage truck came by. After many trips between
the house and the garbage collection corner, they
had managed to get rid of almost everything. All
that remained in Amiko's possession were a few

pairs of underwear and clothes, two pencils and a writing pad, three keychains, a walkie-talkie, a brand-new set of toothbrush and toothpaste, and an old handkerchief.

The electric heater blazed at her feet, and as Amiko twisted her legs away from the heat, she suddenly heard the familiar sound again. *Psss, kurrrr, cluck.* She raised herself up, covered her mouth, and listened. Yes, she could hear the sound from the balcony just next to her head, beyond the glass door. I'll sing the song again, she decided. She was used to this by now. Singing was the solution. She opened her mouth and inhaled. Then suddenly she felt a choking sensation in the back of her throat. She didn't understand what was happening.

Gsss gsssss gsss, grrr, brrr brrr, ssh ssh. The sound grew louder and louder outside the glass door.

Amiko couldn't speak. It wasn't only her voice. She couldn't breathe either. She couldn't figure out whether she wanted to inhale or exhale. It's the spirit, she thought. She still believed in it. She didn't know whose spirit it was—and even if she did, she couldn't make another grave. The last time she made one it made someone cry. There was nothing she could do.

Amiko curled her body into a fetal position. The sound was shaking her body. Her heart beat fast from deep inside to the sound coming from the balcony. She felt pain in her chest and she couldn't breathe. Her body shook more and more violently. She was unable to stand up. The deafening noise assaulted her.

I'm gonna die, Amiko thought. Then, at that moment, in the middle of her utter confusion, she realized something.

The deafening sound wasn't coming from the balcony. It wasn't coming from inside her either. It was another sound, coming from an entirely different place. This new sound was so loud that it shoved aside the spirit and her heartbeat. Yes, she recognized it now. The deafening, explosive sound shook Amiko's head and body; it shook the entire room. It came from far away with great force, ranting and raging, going berserk, trampling and crushing all the other sounds that had assailed Amiko. Trampling and crushing.

It was the sound of Saturday night. It was the sound of the engine, that fierce and crazy engine that she'd heard every weekend night. It rarely showed itself, but roared and rampaged at breakneck speed without a care about anything.

Then suddenly it became quiet. The sound of the engine ceased. Amiko inhaled through her trembling mouth, then exhaled. She could breathe again. She reached out and pulled the pink box toward her with both hands. She slid open the lid and gently pulled out an old discolored toy. She wanted to talk to someone. She pressed the round, yellow button. She put it to her ear, expecting to hear a buzzing sound. But there was nothing. Still, Amiko uttered the words:

"Do you copy? Do you copy? This is Amiko."

There was no response from anyone or anywhere.

"Do you copy? Do you copy? This is Amiko. This is Amiko. Do you copy?" No matter how many times she called out, there was no response.

"Um, are you listening? It's me, Amiko."

She decided to talk to herself.

"Dad and Mom are getting a divorce. I'm gonna move out with Dad, so I won't be staying in this house for too long. It's goodbye to the neighbors."

Even as she said this, she couldn't recall a single neighbor's face.

"It's goodbye to Nori, too," she continued. "Nori cried the other day. He cried. Told me not to tell anyone, so I didn't."

Amiko hadn't been to school since that day.

She sighed into her unresponsive walkie-talkie and ran her tongue along her gums where the teeth were missing.

"And you know what, it was a baby sister, not a brother. How come no one told me? They never tell me anything. Nobody ever tells me anything."

The walkie-talkie felt hot. Amiko's hands were sweaty. The tatami room filled with the laughter of her classmates. Why were they laughing? It was because Amiko was crying. When Amiko cried, everyone laughed. You look weird when you cry. They roared with laughter, pointing their fingers at her. Was it really so funny? Amiko couldn't tell.

"Ahhh."

Was it so funny?

"Ahhh... there's the spirit. There it is now. I can't take it anymore..."

Then, as she said this, her ears caught a fragment of a word. It was the first response that came from within the walkie-talkie, which had lost its function. It was gone in a moment, but she had heard it. In a very low, quiet voice, a single word—"Huh?"

Amiko swallowed hard and tried again.

"There's a ghost... on the balcony." When she uttered those words, a sense of dread suddenly welled up inside her and she couldn't stop. "What do I do? I'm scared, I'm scared. I'm so so so so scared. I'm scared, oh I'm so scared. Help me... KOTA!"

A thundering sound passed through her legs, and with a sharp bang the sliding door to her room burst open. Amiko looked up and saw a lion-like figure standing before her. The lion stood firm and nodded to Amiko, who sat there with her mouth hanging open. Then the lion stepped into the room.

Amiko knew that this was not their first meeting. She had known this person since birth. But she couldn't make the connection in her mind, no matter what. He's the one, she thought to herself. This person, who stood like a grand animal in the glittering dust washed in the winter sunlight. He was Tanaka-senpai.

Tanaka-senpai passed in front of Amiko and put his hand on the glass door. Amiko sat on the tatami, gazing at his golden mane and magnificent clothes covered in complex kanji. The door slid open with a loud bang. This was followed by a deafening, clanging sound. It was the sound of a stack of flowerpots getting kicked over. Amiko cried out, and at the same moment a dark thing flew across the balcony, making a loud rustling sound.

It was a bird. What kind of bird it was, Amiko didn't know. It had flapped its wings and flown away quickly. Amiko crawled on all fours to the glass door and nervously stuck her head out onto the balcony. The cold wind whipped her forehead as she looked around. Following Tanaka-senpai's gaze, she saw, tucked among the broken flowerpots, a bird's nest. The nest was about the size of Amiko's palms spread out. It was just like the ones in the picture books she'd read as a child, with three small eggs nestled in the center. *Wow*, Amiko whispered, and moved closer to get a better look. *How long have you been here, little eggs? Are you gonna hatch soon?* Her heart pounded and overflowed with words she wanted to say to the eggs. *That bird that just flew away. Is she your mom? Don't worry, she'll be back soon. She'll know to come home. This balcony is yours. Don't be afraid. There's nothing to worry about.* Amiko reached out her hand to gently stroke the eggs. But just before her fingers touched the nest, they were intercepted by a large hand that was covered in scars. By the time she realized what was happening it was too late. Tanaka-senpai's hand grabbed the nest with the eggs in it. There was a dry, crackling sound, and twigs spilled out from between his thick fingers. Clutching the nest with his bare hands, he looked up at the sky. Amiko followed his eyes and looked to the sky too. Then, in the next moment,

Ooorah!

With a bellowing roar, Tanaka-senpai hurled the nest and eggs high, high up into the air. Amiko, unable to utter a word, just looked on.

In the crisp winter air she watched, with wide-open eyes, until they disintegrated at the highest point in the sky.

In the back of the classroom, the calligraphy work of all the students was exhibited on the wall. Amiko's was not there. Maybe she was absent that day. Amiko didn't see Nori anywhere, so she asked a boy passing by which one was Nori's.

"Not again," the boy replied as he flicked a sheet of paper with his finger. On the sheet was written 金鳳花.

"You ask me every time which one is Nori's," the boy laughed. "You have a one-track mind."

Amiko asked the boy how to read the kanji.

"*Kinpougé*. It means buttercup," he said.

"Oh, weird. That's his last name?" Amiko asked.

There was a pause, and the boy turned his head toward her. "What... you mean Washio? Is that what you wanna know? Washio?" He looked at Amiko in disbelief.

"Huh? Washio? I don't understand."

"Yeah, Washio is your love crush Nori."

"So what's this bittercup then?"

"You stupid. Buttercup is this kanji in the center. It's the name of a flower."

Next to the word for a flower she had never heard of, Amiko saw the words: *Washio Yoshinori, Year Three, Class Three.*

This was what Amiko wanted to know. They'd been in the same class in the first and second grade of elementary school, then again in the first and third years of junior high school. She must have seen Nori's name countless times, but the kanji were too difficult for Amiko, who avoided studying. The characters looked familiar, but she couldn't read them. She made up her mind to know them from now on.

"Hey, by the way, this one's my name. Can you read it? You can read it, right?" The boy pointed to another sheet. The kanji were messy, and Amiko quickly looked away. She was too busy repeating Washio Yoshinori to answer the boy's question—鷲尾佳範. These kanji were a little easier, a little kinder, than those written on Tanaka-senpai's clothes.

"Hard to believe we're finally graduating," the boy, who was still there, said softly. He started whistling, then stopped, then started humming. It was a melody Amiko had heard before. She opened her mouth to sing along, but the humming had already stopped. The boy asked her if she was going to high school. It was the first time anyone had asked her such a question.

"Nope," Amiko replied.

"Hmmm. What are you gonna do then?"

"I'm moving to my grandma's during spring break. We're gonna grow peaches together." It was her grandmother on Father's side of the family. She was gentle and old and could only move slowly. "Are you going to high school?" she asked the boy.

"You bet. I'm going to a school in Sendai on a baseball scholarship. Isn't that cool?"

"Ah, sure."

"If you studied a little harder, you could've gone to high school too."

"You think so?"

"Sure, you could have."

"Hmmm."

"Of course you could have."

"I don't know."

"Hey."

"What?"

"You could've done it."

"Uh huh," Amiko murmured.

"Anyway, we've known each other for a long time, but I guess this is it. We'll finally go our separate ways."

Amiko didn't understand what he meant. She looked up at his face and examined it carefully. The boy had a shaved head and a tan, even though it was winter. Tall, tanned boys with shaved heads all looked the same to her.

"Hmm... You must be somebody that knows me well, huh?" she said, pointing at the shaved head.

"What are you talking about? You know me well too."

"I don't know you."

"Drop dead," said the shaved head, laughing. Amiko laughed too. "The only person you ever see is Washio, isn't it? No matter how creepy he thought you were, you never gave up. Ever since elementary school. That's amazing." The shaved head patted Amiko on the shoulder, as if to congratulate her.

"He thought I was creepy?" Amiko asked.

The shaved head was silent for a moment. But his smile soon returned. "Well... maybe you just pestered him too much."

"Tell me what was creepy about me though."

"What was creepy about you? I can tell you a billion examples."

"Okay, tell me."

"You want me to tell you one by one? From the beginning? Should I write them down and make you a chart?"

"From the beginning."

"Well... it's hard to say what exactly..."

"So...?"

The smiling face of the shaved head suddenly became solemn. From his expression, Amiko understood that he knew how serious she was. She looked him in the eye once more and said, "I wanna know."

The shaved head didn't look away. After a short silence, he finally opened his mouth. "Well..." With a stiff expression he continued, "That's... for me to know."

His expression was firm, but his eyes wandered. Amiko searched for words. Anything to say to those eyes. She wanted to be kind. But the more she wanted to be kind, the sadder she got. She couldn't find the words. She couldn't say a word.

Father hadn't exactly lied. He'd asked Amiko if she wanted to move, but he never said anything about moving together. He also never said anything about a divorce.

Amiko forgot a lot of faces she used to know. Some of them, she didn't even know their names to begin with.

"Don't forget me after we graduate," the shaved head said to Amiko as he poked her on the shoulder. He walked out of the classroom without waiting for her reply. She was glad she didn't promise not to forget him. Because she already had.

It was the beginning of summer, and Amiko stood waiting outside Grandmother's house for her little friend to arrive on stilts. The child's shadow swayed in the sunlight and didn't seem to be getting any closer.

"Ami-chan, dear."

Amiko was being called.

"Ami-chan. Oh, sweetheart."

Amiko dropped the bag with the violets, surprised to hear her name, and wakened from her thoughts. "Yes, Grandma!" she called out, and headed toward the house where the voice was coming from. On her way in Amiko turned around, but started walking forward again. It's all right. The little girl won't get here anytime soon.

MORE FROM PUSHKIN'S JAPANESE NOVELLA SERIES

KAORI FUJINO

NAILS AND EYES

KAZUSHIGE ABE

NIPPONIA NIPPON

NATSUKO IMAMURA
AUTHOR OF THE WOMAN IN THE PURPLE SKIRT

THIS IS AMIKO, DO YOU COPY?

NISHIOKA KYŌDAI

KAFKA

TOH ENJOE

HARLEQUIN BUTTERFLY

KUMI KIMURA

SOMEONE TO WATCH OVER YOU

JAPANESE FICTION
AVAILABLE AND COMING SOON
FROM PUSHKIN PRESS

MS ICE SANDWICH
Mieko Kawakami

MURDER IN THE AGE OF ENLIGHTENMENT
Ryūnosuke Akutagawa

THE HONJIN MURDERS
Seishi Yokomizo

RECORD OF A NIGHT TOO BRIEF
Hiromi Kawakami

SPRING GARDEN
Tomoka Shibasaki

COIN LOCKER BABIES
Ryu Murakami

THE DECAGON HOUSE MURDERS
Yukito Ayatsuji

SLOW BOAT
Hideo Furukawa

THE HUNTING GUN
Yasushi Inoue

SALAD ANNIVERSARY
Machi Tawara

THE CAKE TREE IN THE RUINS
Akiyuki Nosaka